Jeb Scarecrow's Pumpkin Patch

Jeb Scarecrow's Pumpkin Patch

JANA DILLON

Houghton Mifflin Company
Boston

For my children, Brian Byrne Doherty
and Alison Meghan Doherty, with love

Library of Congress Cataloging-in-Publication Data

Dillon, Jana.
  Jeb Scarecrow's pumpkin patch / Jana Dillon.
    p.   cm.
    Summary: Jeb Scarecrow comes up with a wonderful plan to
scare the crows away from his pumpkin patch.
  RNF 0-395-57578-8   PAP ISBN 0-395-74514-4
  [1. Scarecrows — Fiction. 2. Pumpkin — Fiction.
3. Crows — Fiction. 4. Jack-o-lanterns — Fiction.]
I. Title.
PZ7.D5795Je   1992   91-16423
[E] — dc20   CIP
                               AC

Printed in the United States of America
BVG 20 19 18 17 16 15 14 13 12 11

It's mighty hard work scaring crows all day. Crows don't scare easy. A scarecrow's got to flap and wave his arms around, and kick and hurl his legs. He's got to look like a wild man before he can scare those pesky, seed-guzzling, fruit-pecking crows.

Jeb Scarecrow was just a kid, but he did a fine job guarding his family's pumpkin patch. Those pumpkin seeds had sprouted up all around him right nicely last spring. Now they were huge orange pumpkins basking in the October sun.

In the evenings, when the crows were in their nests, Jeb ambled along home to the little straw cottage he shared with Mommo and Daddo in the woods at the edge of the pumpkin patch.

"Jeb, I've got bad news for you, son," Mommo said that night at dinner. "There's talk among the crows of a big harvest celebration right in your pumpkin patch the week before Halloween."

Jeb dropped his fork. "Why me?" he cried. "Why now?"

"Those crazy crows throw a party every year, son," said Daddo. "So far it's been in other scarecrows' pumpkin patches. This year they chose yours."

"They'll peck and pick at all my pumpkins," wailed Jeb. "I won't be able to sell any for Halloween. Dawgone it, what am I going to do?"

"Not much you can do, son," said Daddo, shaking his head sadly. "No scarecrow ever won out over the crows when it comes to their harvest bash. No, sir. Not one scarecrow ever won."

"There's no way around it, Jeb," said Mommo with a sigh. "Your pumpkin patch is as good as gone right now. You might as well forget it. There's always next year."

"Nope. They just can't have it. Not *my* pumpkin patch!" said Jeb, and he stabbed his fork angrily into his cherry pie.

Each day, Jeb Scarecrow stubbornly showed up in the pumpkin patch at dawn's first light. He tried to plot some way to save his pumpkins, but it took a lot of thought, and the crows didn't leave Jeb much time for deep thinking.

"You're not partying here," Jeb warned Grandfather Crow as he swooped by.

"Oh, yes, we are," cawed Grandfather Crow. "And no scarecrow can stop us. Least of all *you,* Jeb Scarecrow. You're nothing but a kid." And he flew away, laughing, "Haw, haw, haw!"

"No one is celebrating in *my* pumpkin patch," Jeb yelled at Bernie Crow.

"You wait and see, Jeb Scarecrow," mocked Bernie. "This pumpkin patch will be nothing but leftovers." And he flew away, chanting, "PARty! PARty! PARty!"

"You crows should celebrate in the wild, not in some hard-working scarecrow's patch," Jeb scolded Lucy Crow.

"And eat berries when we could be eating giant juicy pumpkins? No thanks!" said Lucy Crow saucily. "We're going to eat *pumpkins.* That's right. *These* pumpkins. *Your* pumpkins!"

There's not a scarecrow alive who doesn't get nervous the night before he has to do something important. The night before the crows' big bash, Jeb tossed and turned and twirled until his sheets were twisted all around his middle.

It was his last chance to think of a plan. He thought of this, he thought of that. He got up three times to eat.

At last, in the darkest hour of night, Jeb hatched a plot.

Never mind not much sleep, Jeb was up at dawn. As soon as Mommo and Daddo heard him, they leaped out of bed.

Jeb told them of his plan.

"We'll help, Jeb," said Mommo, "any way we can."

All day long the crows kept Mommo and Daddo running up and
down the pumpkin patch while Jeb worked steadily.

He covered some of his pumpkins with a shirt, a shawl, or some other piece of clothing, then mysteriously crawled under each one.

"Give up, Jeb," jeered Grandfather Crow. "We crows will win. You lose, we win. You lose, we win. We win, loser! Haw!"

"What are you doing so sneaky-like under those clothes?" asked Lucy Crow.

But Jeb didn't bother to answer. He kept on working.

At sunset, Daddo shouted, "Jeb! The neighborhood crows have flown away to meet their guests!"

Jeb jumped out from under a scarf and said, "Mommo! Daddo! Quick! We've got to set up the last part of my plan!"

The sky still glowed in the twilight, but the earth was dark and shadowy when the scarecrow family was finished.

"I sure hope this works," whispered Mommo.

"Cross your fingers," Daddo said softly.

"Here they come!" whooped Jeb.

The sky darkened with noisy birds.

"Wait till you see these mouth-watering pumpkins!" Bernie Crow cawed loudly to the guests following him. "Yessir! PARty time!"

"We're almost there!" Lucy Crow shouted.

But as they came over the tops of the trees to Jeb Scarecrow's pumpkin patch, Bernie Crow hollered, "Hold everything!"

"Monsters!" shrieked Lucy Crow. "Guarding Jeb Scarecrow's pumpkin patch!"

Great orange heads, staring like spooks, grinned up at them wickedly from the pumpkin patch. "Turn back!" squawked Bernie Crow. The neighborhood crows tried to stop, but the crows behind them just kept coming.

Soon the crows were all banging into each other, cawing and
screeching, feathers flying everywhere.

"Turn back!" shouted Lucy Crow. "That pumpkin patch is haunted!"

"Stop pushing!" hollered Grandfather crow. "Let an old crow
through!"

"Party's over!" cawed Bernie Crow. "Party's *over*!"

As the crows disappeared over the trees, Jeb collapsed with laughter. Mommo and Daddo sat down beside him, heehawing till their sides hurt.

The honking of a car horn silenced their laughter.

"Hey, Mr. Scarecrow," called a fellow from his car. "I'll buy one of those jack-o'-lanterns for Halloween. I couldn't carve one better myself. And I'll want one of those plain pumpkins, too, for pie."

A car pulled up behind his, and then another.

Soon the street was lined with cars. Folks were waving money and smiling at the jack-o'-lanterns and the pumpkins.

Jeb was smiling, too, as he and Mommo and Daddo hurried about, selling his darling pumpkins.